Hickory Dickory Dock

Story by:
Michelle Baron

Illustrated by:

Theresa Mazurek	Rivka
Douglas McCarthy	Fay Whitemountain
Allyn Conley-Gorniak	Su-Zan
Lorann Downer	Lisa Souza
	Julie Armstrong

This Book Belongs To:

Use this symbol to match book and cassette.

The name of this nursery rhyme is "Hickory, Dickory, Dock." It goes like this:

Hickory, Dickory, Dock,
The mouse ran up the clock,
The clock struck one,
The mouse ran down,
Hickory, Dickory, Dock.

Hector wanted to learn how to tell time.
So he started on the path to the village
to find the mouse who could teach him.
When he reached a fork in the road,
he saw something unexpected–a little
mouse carrying a knapsack.

So Hector asked the travelling mouse
if he knew where he could find the
"Hickory, Dickory, Dock" mouse.

To Hector's surprise, that mouse was the "Hickory, Dickory, Dock" mouse. His name was Murray.

Now Murray said that he'd be very happy to teach Hector how to tell time, as soon as they found a clock. In fact, he wanted to find lots of clocks and that's why he was on his way to the village. You see, Murray had lived in the same grandfather clock for a long time, and he'd grown rather tired of it.

Murray knew that there were many
different kinds of clocks, but he had only
heard of such clocks. Now, he thought,
was the time to actually see them.

"The Clock Song"

Chorus

Clocks, clocks, they always work,
And they never stop to play.
Clocks, clocks are everywhere.
You see them here,
You see them there,
Tick-tocking through the day.
They never stop to play.

They can be big on a wall,
Or they can be small.
They can tell us it's time for a date.
They can fit in your pocket,
Or inside a locket.
If you can tell time
You'll never be late!

They can hang from a chain.
Can they tell it's going to rain?
No, they don't tell what's going to be—
They tell us the now.
I want to know how to tell time.
Teach me, please?

Repeat Chorus
It's simply alarming,
There is nothing as charming
As a tick of a resounding tock.
Below or above,
You can't help but love,
The sound of your very own clock!

Repeat Chorus
Tick-tocking through the day.

So Hector and Murray headed toward the village together. For a long time they saw only trees. Then they saw cobblestone streets and shop signs. They had arrived in the village.

Now Murray heard something familiar. They followed the sound, and it grew louder and louder.

The sound was coming from a clock store. Hector and Murray stood looking through the shop window. They were amazed! Murray rubbed his eyes in disbelief, for there in front of him was every kind of clock he had ever heard of, and some he hadn't.

Hector and Murray went into the store. Murray looked at all the clocks inside and out. He looked at the pendulums and the springs, the dials and the gears. Murray thought he was having more fun than he could ever have had living in that old grandfather clock.

Then Hector's time-telling lesson began.

Murray told Hector that there are twelve numbers on the clock.

Then Murray told Hector that there is a big hand and a little hand.

The hands point to the numbers.

Then Murray jumped onto a clock and continued the lesson.

Murray pushed the little hand around the clockface so it pointed to each number. He explained that each number meant an hour. Hector caught on quickly.

Then it was time for a "test." Murray pointed to another clock across the room.

Hector could tell the time alright. It was twelve o'clock! Murray knew what that meant. At the stroke of twelve every clock in the shop chimed and buzzed and whistled and rang! The noise was loud and alarming. Murray and Hector ran out of the clock shop and kept running until they reached the very same spot where they had met.

After all the noise of the clock shop, Murray could think of only one thing– his grandfather clock. Its quiet "tick-tocks" and its lovely chimes seemed to call to him.

Hector was happy. He had finally learned to tell time and he could hardly wait to tell me. So both friends agreed that it was time to go home.

"It's Time To Go Home"

Home is where your heart is,
At least that's what they say.
But to me my clock is home-sweet-home,
And that is where I'll stay.

Chorus

It's time to go home.
Let's call it a day.
We've done quite a lot.
There's no more to say.
Back in my room
I can have quiet play.
It's time to go home.
Let's call it a day.

I've heard the clocks chime,
I've learned to tell time.
We've had fun in town,
Now it's time to slow down.

Because back in my house,
I'm a cozy little mouse.
And back in my nest,
I'll be happy to rest.

Repeat Chorus

Hector and Murray said their good-byes and they headed down their separate paths toward home. Hector came running into my house.

Just then the clock struck one.

Hector smiled. He knew that it was one o'clock, and he knew that Murray was running down his grandfather clock. He knew that Murray was happy, and he knew that Murray was home.